MY VILLAGE

Rhymes from around the World

Collected by Danielle Wright

Illustrated by Mique Moriuchi

Introduced by Michael Rosen

F

FRANCES LINCOLN
CHILDREN'S BOOKS

Illustrations © Mique Moriuchi
First published in Australia and New Zealand in 2008 by
Gecko Press, PO Box 9335
Marion Square, Wellington 6141, New Zealand
info@geckopress.com

First published in Great Britain and in the USA in 2010 by
Frances Lincoln Children's Books, 4 Torriano Mews,
Torriano Avenue, London NW5 2RZ
www.franceslincoln.com

A catalogue record for this book is available from the British Library.

ISBN: 978-1-84780-086-2

Special thanks to Ruby Hammond, Sigbjørn Obstfelder, Iben Nagel Rasmussen on behalf of
Halfdan Rasmussen, Farideh Khalatbaree, for permission to print their poems.
We would also like to thank translators Aida Nofrita, Andrea Gardi, Anjana Mani, Carim Portella,
Farideh Khalatbaree, Genia Gurarie, Hallberg Hallmundsson, Katrien Vander Straeten,
Lisa Yanucci, Monique Palomares, Mavis Kumbala-Mutisi, Nora Yao, Paul Selver, Rob Amery,
Sereima Lumelume, Wanda Cowley, Wilma van den Bosch, Winifred Mahowa.

Printed in Singapore by Tien Wah Press (Pte) Ltd in December 2010

9 8 7 6 5 4 3 2

For Gavin and Henry

CONTENTS

INTRODUCTION

Books of Nursery Rhymes first appeared in the mid-seventeenth century in England. The first known collection was called *Tommy Thumb's Pretty Song Book* and there were two volumes, though the first has never been found! But what are Nursery Rhymes? They are a strange mix of poems: some are fragments of longer songs and ballads, some are rhymes that were probably oral jingles or chants that people sang or said to their children, a small group are carefully composed little poems with known authors, and some are songs that always accompanied dancing or actions of some kind. There have been two intellectual sports connected to the rhymes: trying to find the 'real' personages that the rhymes are about; trying to find the uncensored versions of the rhymes. So it is that people will claim that Georgie Porgie is one of the King Georges of England or that the rhyme about pulling fishes out of eyes is really about something else altogether. In fact, no one has ever proved these theories and almost certainly never will.

What this leaves us is the rhymes themselves. They are tiny short stories, full of random acts of violence, loss, greed and mishap. The characters are abruptly drawn, either thrown into an action without explanation, or impelled by one bold urge. They are full of verbal fun and absurdity which matches the impossible deeds we often read about. If we learn them when we're very young, they can become our companions for life. I, for one, can remember my feeling that I knew that old man who bumps his head and can't get up in the morning. He lived on our street. Now, some sixty years later, he's me! In between, the Mary Mary quite contrarys I thought I knew at school became transformed into girls I've helped bring up.

All this is of course an English language tradition, which, incidentally, was very vigorous in the early days of the United States of America. Other cultures and languages possess their small-scale rhymes intended for children and I've heard such poems or songs from France, Germany, Turkey, Bangladesh and West Africa. But I've never heard them translated in a way that makes them accessible to an English-speaking audience, so I'm looking forward to reading and re-reading this book and perhaps I'll have some new companions with me.

Michael Rosen

BIG WHALE

Big whale,
Long whale,
Very fat whale,
Swish your tail, whale
Spout your blowhole, whale
Whale swimming in the sea.

NEW ZEALAND

TOHORĀ NUI

Tohorā nui
Tohorā roa
Tohorā tino mōmona
Tohorā whiuwhiua
Tohorā pupuha
Tohorā kaukau i te moana e.

9

LITTLE FRIENDS, HAND IN HAND

Little Monkey wants a friend,
Shakes hands with little Pig;
Hand in hand, hand in hand,
Monkey walks with Piglet.

Little Pig wants a friend,
Shakes hands with little Pup;
Hand in hand, hand in hand,
Piglet walks with Puppy.

Finding friends, shaking hands,
Monkey, Piglet, Puppy;
Hand in hand, hand in hand,
All become good friends!

小朋友，勾勾手

小猴小猴找朋友，

见到小猪勾勾手；

勾勾手，勾勾手，

小猪跟着小猴走。

小猪小猪找朋友，

见到小狗勾勾手；

勾勾手，勾勾手，

小狗跟着小猪走。

找朋友，伸出手，

伸出手，勾勾手；

小猴小猪和小狗。

大家成了好朋友！

XIAO PENG YOU, GOU GOU SHOU

Xiao hou xiao hou zhao peng you,
Jian dao xiao zhu gou gou shou;
Gou gou shou, gou gou shou,
Xiao zhu gen zhe xiao hou zou.

Xiao zhu xiao zhu zhao peng you,
Jian dao xiao gou gou gou shou;
Gou gou shou, gou gou shou,
Xiao gou gen zhe xiao zhu zou.

Zhao peng you, shen chu shou,
Shen chu shou, gou gou shou;
Xiao hou, xiao zhu he xiao gou,
Da jia cheng le hao peng you!

GRANDFATHER

Grandfather, Grandfather:
Won't you tell me
Stories of our land,
So you can teach me
Who are my people
And from where they came.
Grandfather, Grandfather:
What is my name?

MADLALLA

Madlalla, madlalla:
Ngaiinni wangga
Warra wilta,
Bukkiunungko
Ngana ngaityo birko
Parna wadangko?
Madlalla madlalla:
Ngana ngai narri?

Ruby Hammond and Rob Amery

RAIN

One is one, two is two,
In water we hop,
On sand we drop.
Zick, zack,
Hour after hour,
Tick, tack,
Shower upon shower.

Rain, rain,
Pattering rain,
Rain, rain,
Clattering rain.
Rain, rain,
Little or much,
Rain, rain,
Welcome its touch.

One is one, two is two,
In water we hop,
On sand we drop.
Zick, zack,
Hour after hour,
Tick, tack,
Shower upon shower.

Sigbjørn Obstfelder

REGN

En er en, og to er to,
vi hopper i vand,
vi triller i sand.
Zik zak,
vi drypper på tag,
tik tak,
det regner idag.

Regn, regn, regn, regn,
øsende regn,
pøsende regn,
regn, regn, regn, regn,
deilig og vådt
deilig og råt!

En er en, og to er to,
vi hopper i vand,
vi triller i sand.
Zik zak,
vi drypper på tag,
tik tak,
det regner idag.

15

THE LITTLE DONKEY

I saw a donkey
One day old,
His head was too big
For his neck to hold.

His legs were shaky
Long and loose,
They rocked and staggered
And weren't much use.

He tried to frolic
And frisk a bit,
But he wasn't sure
Of the trick of it.

His scruffy coat
Was soft and grey,
And curled at his neck
In a charming way.

His face was wistful
And left no doubt,
That he felt life needed
Some thinking out.

So he blundered about
On his curious quest,
Then flopped down flat
On the ground to rest.

He looked so little
So weak and slim,
I prayed that the world
Would be good to him.

Elizabeth Shane

SPOTTY SPIDER

Spotty spider give to me
A brand new tooth,
A big and bold one
And in return I'll give to you
My rotten old one!

HINA, HINA

Hina, Hina
mata 'ile 'ila
'omai ho nifo
lelei mo 'oku
kae 'oatu hoku
nifo kovi mo'ou!

TONGA

19

TINGALAY-O!

Tingalay-o!
Come me little donkey, come
Tingalay-o
Come me little donkey, come

Me donkey BUCK
Me donkey LEAP
Me donkey KICK
Wid him two hind feet

Tingalay-o!
Come me little donkey, come
Tingalay-o
Come me little donkey, come

Me donkey WALK
Me donkey TALK
Me donkey EAT
Wid him knife and fork

Tingalay-o!
Come me little donkey, come
Tingalay-o,
Come me little donkey, come

Me donkey HEE
Me donkey HAW
Me donkey SIT
On him kitchen floor

Tingalay-o!

SONG OF KITES

Our kite is rising in the sky
Playful winds will take it high.
Soaring, dancing higher yet
Up where clouds are floating by.

Falling, falling is the kite
Run and run to give it height.
See, our kite is rising now
Don't forget to hold on tight!

TACO NO UTA

Taco taco agare
Kaze yoku ukete.
Kumo made agare
Ten made agare.

Edako ni jidako
Dochira mo makezu.
Kumo made agare
Ten made agare.

Are are sagaru
Hike hike ito wo.
Are are agaru
Hanasu na ito wo.

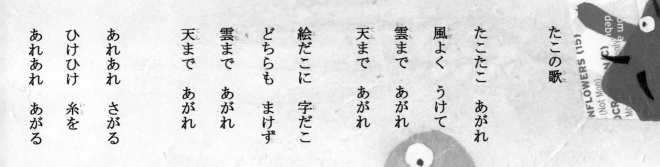

三
あれあれ　さがる
ひけひけ　糸を
あれあれ　あがる

二
絵だこに　字だこ
どちらも　まけず
雲まで　あがれ
天まで　あがれ

一
たこたこ　あがれ
風よく　うけて
雲まで　あがれ
天まで　あがれ

たこの歌

23

BEAUTIFUL BIRD

Beautiful bird where are you going?
Come, come, come let's play.
I'm going to the clouds,
I want to be like the clouds.

SHIRI YAKANAKA

Shiri yakanaka unoendepi?
Huya huya huya titambe.
Ndiri kuenda kumakore.
Kuti ndifanane nemakore.

ZIMBABWE

TAPIOCA

Eat, be merry
Eat, be merry
Ta..pi..oca
Ta..pi..oca
Fishy with the veges
Fishy with the veges
Yum, yum, yum
Yum, yum, yum

(to the tune of 'Frère Jacques')

TAVIOKA

Kana mada
kana mada
tavioka
tavioka
kena i coi na bele
kena i coi na bele
na ika
na ika

27

MY VILLAGE

My village that I love
My village, my sweet home
Where my father, mother and family live
It's not easy to forget it
It's so hard to be away
My peaceful, friendly village
I miss it every day.

DESAKU

Desaku yang kucinta
Pujaan hatiku
Tempat ayah dan bunda
Dan handai taulanku
Tak mudah kulupakan
Tak mudah tercerai
Selalu kurindukan
Desaku yang permai.

INDONESIA

29

SNOWMAN FROST

Snowman Frost and Lady Thaw
Went for walks and thought of more.
Found a garden seat and sat,
Talked of love and this and that.

Snowman Frost, a little weak,
Asked her, "May I kiss your cheek?"
But as Lady Thaw grew warm
He began to lose his form.

As their passion rose in heat
Off he melted from the seat.
When he kissed her tender lips
He slipped through her fingertips.

All alone without 'amore'
On the seat sits Lady Thaw.
Snowman Frost no more will hug;
She must keep him in a mug!

SNEMAND FROST

Snemand Frost og Frøken Tø
gik en tur ved Søndersø
fandt en bænk og slog sig ned,
talte lidt om kærlighed.

Snemand Frost, som var lidt bleg,
spurgte: "Må jeg kysse dig?"
Men da frøken Tø var varm
smeltede hans højre arm.

Da han kyssed' hendes kind,
svandt han ganske langsomt ind.
Da han kyssed' hendes mund
blev han væk i samme stund.

På en bænk ved Søndersø
sidder stakkelts frøken Tø.
Snemand Frost er smeltet op;
Hun må ha ham i en kop!

31

LET'S PLAY

I'm a ball, soft and round,
Throw and catch me, up and down;
Play with me till bedtime.

I'm a slide, tall and steep,
Climb and slide back to my feet;
Shout for joy till bedtime.

I'm a swing, swift and high,
Let me swing you to the sky;
Laugh and talk till bedtime.

I'm a leg, kind and fat,
Stretch me out or fold me back;
Bounce on me till bedtime.

I'm a toy, your cuddly dad,
You can ride me piggyback;
Come along, it's bedtime.

MAN HAM BAZI

Man yek toop am, bozorg,
Bala va paeen miparam, tond va tond.
Ba man bazi kon, ta vaghte khab.

Man yek sorsoreh am, boland,
Benshin va sor bokhor.
As man harf bezan, ta vaghte khab.

Man yek tab am, mohkam,
Negaham dar va boro bala va paeen.
Be man fekr kon, ta vaghte khab.

Man yek pay am, kotah,
Deraz mishavam, baraye atal matal,
Sandali mishavam, ta vaghte khab.

Man yek asbabbazi am, male to,
Savarat mikonam, roye doosham.
Baba, Baba bego, ta vaghte khab.

من هم بازی

من یک توپم ، بزرگ ،
بالا و پایین می‌پرم ، تند و تند د
با من بازی کن ، تا وقت خواب د

من یک سرسره‌ام ، بلند ،
بنشین و سر بخور ، هزار بار د
از من حرف بزن ، تا وقت خواب د

من یک جای قایم شدنم ، کوچک ،
قایم باشک بازی کن ، بی‌صدا د
چشمهایت را ببند و بشمار ، تا وقت خواب د

من یک تابم ، محکم ،
نگاهم دار و برو ، بالا و پایین د
به من فکر کن ، تا وقت خواب د

من یک الاکلنگم ، دراز ،
مواظب خودت باش ، در هوا د
همبازیم بمان ، تا وقت خواب د

من یک سنگم ، قل قلی ،
یک قل دو قل بازی کن ، در اتاق د
پرتم کن و بگیر ، تا وقت خواب د

من یک پایم ، کوتاه ،
دراز می‌شوم ، برای اتل متل د
صندلی می‌شوم ، تا وقت خواب د

من یک اسباب بازیم ، مال تو ،
سوارت می‌کنم ، روی دوشم د
بابا ، بابا بگو ، تا وقت خواب د

33

DANCE, LITTLE ONE, DANCE!

Dance, little one, dance around,
Let your shoes fly over the ground.
If they should break, then never fear,
The cobbler will make you another pair.
Just dance, little one, dance!

TANZ, KINDLEIN, TANZ!

Tanz, Kindlein, tanz!
Die Schuhe sind noch ganz.
Laß dich's nicht gereuen,
Der Schuster macht dir neue,
Tanz, Kindlein, tanz!

SAVALIVALI

Savalivali means go for a walk
Tele tautala means too much talk
Alofa ia te oe means I love you
Hey, take it easy: *fai fai lemu*.

Teine aulelei means pretty girl
Ta'amilomilo means around the world
Whisper to me: *musumusu mai*
Oi aue! My, oh my!

SAMOA

JOGGELI, CAN YOU RIDE?

Joggeli, can you ride?
Yes, yes, yes.
Have you got one leg each side?
Yes, yes, yes.
Did you give the horse some hay?
Yes, yes, yes.
Did you water it today?
Nay, nay, nay.

So let's ride to the fountain
And go three times around.
But then the horse starts bucking
And Joggeli falls down
      down
         down.

JOGGELI, CHASCH AU RITE?

Joggeli, chasch au rite?
 Ja, ja, ja.
   Hesch beidi Bei uf de Site?
   Ja, ja, ja.
    Hesch am Rössli Hafer geh?
    Ja, ja, ja.
     Hesch am Rössli z'trinke geh?
     Nei, nei, nei.

     Denn ritemer zum Brunne
      Und ritet drü Mal rundume.
       Dunn machts Rössli 'trap trap'
        Und de Joggeli gheit
         hine abe…
          hine abe.

39

HUSH YOU MICE

Hush you mice! a cat is near us,
He can see us, he can hear us.
– What if he is on a diet? –
Even then you should be quiet!

RUSSIA

TISHE, MYSHI

Tishe, myshi, kot na kryshe.
On ne vidit i ne slyshit.
Mysh, vedi sebia prilichno,
Zanimaysia na otlichno.

ТИШЕ, МЫШИ

Тише, мыши, кот на крыше.
Он не видит и не слышит.
Мышь, веди себя прилично,
Занимайся на отлично.

41

IF THIS STREET WERE MINE

In this street there is a forest
And I call it Solitude.
In the forest is an angel
One who stole away my heart.

If I stole, I stole your heart
It's because you've stolen mine.
If I stole, I stole your heart
That's because – I love you.

If this street, this street were mine
I would pave this street with tiles.
Little tiles of diamond stone
For you, my love, to walk upon.

SE ESTA RUA FOSSE MINHA

Nesta rua, nesta rua, tem um bosque
Que se chama, que se chama, Solidão.
Dentro dele, dentro dele mora um anjo
Que roubou, que roubou meu coração.

Se eu roubei, se eu roubei seu coração
É porque tu roubastes o meu também.
Se eu roubei, se eu roubei teu coração
É porque eu te quero tanto bem.

Se esta rua se esta rua fosse minha
Eu mandava, eu mandava ladrilhar.
Com pedrinhas, com pedrinhas
          de brilhante
Para o meu, para o meu amor passar.

WHAT IS MY HAND DOING?

What is my hand doing?
It strokes: soft, soft, soft
It pinches: sharp, sharp, sharp
It tickles: squirm, squirm, squirm
It bangs: boom, boom, boom
It dances: swirl, swirl, swirl
And then . . . it's gone!

44

QUE FAIT MA MAIN?

Que fait ma main?
Elle caresse: doux, doux, doux
Elle pince: ouille, ouille, ouille
Elle chatouille: guili, guili, guili
Elle gratte: gre, gre, gre
Elle frappe: pan, pan, pan
Elle danse: hop, hop, hop
Et puis . . . elle s'en va!

KORTJAKJE IS ALWAYS SICK

Kortjakje is always sick
In the middle of the week
Never on a Sunday though;
Sunday's when she goes to church
With her book of silver work.

Kortjakje is always sick
In the middle of the week
Never on a Sunday though;
On Sundays she is always well
Because her true love comes to call.

Kortjakje is always sick
In the middle of the week
But never on a Sunday.

(to the tune of 'Twinkle Twinkle
Little Star')

ALTIJD IS KORTJAKJE ZIEK

Altijd is Kortjakje ziek
Midden in de week maar 's zondags niet
's Zondags gaat zij naar de kerk
Met een boek vol zilverwerk

Altijd is Kortjakje ziek
Midden in de week maar 's zondags niet
's Zondags als haar liefste komt
Is Kortjakje goed gezond

Altijd is Kortjakje ziek
Midden in de week maar 's zondags niet

HOLLAND

47

48

BYE, BYE, BLACKING

Bye, bye, Blacking,
Swans are a-clacking.
I pretend I'm fast asleep,
Even though I'm wide awake.

Round and round the bramble,
Sleepy children ramble
All along the mountain ridge
Looking for their lambs.

BÍ BÍ OG BLAKA

Bí, bí og blaka,
álftirnar kvaka,
ég læt sem ég sofi,
en samt mun ég vaka.

Bíum, bíum bamba,
börnin litlu þamba,
fram á fjallakamba
að leita sér lamba.

49

BATHTIME

My darling is so well behaved;
On the tub he sits and bathes.
The crooked tub tips side to side,
– a rocking horse for him to ride.
Sleep, my darling, sleep.

NAWANU WAKAR

Bhai maro dhaiyo;
patla basi naiyo.
Patla nu pug toh koro,
bhai na rumwa joiya gorro.
Aahli, aahli, aahli.

CREDITS AND ACKNOWLEDGMENTS

Page 8 New Zealand *Big Whale*
For Ngaira Hay (Nana). Thanks to John Archer from www.folksong.org.nz and to Melinda Butt at APRA/AMCOS for copyright information. Thanks to Fiona McIntyre and Kindercare Learning Centres, Milford, for help with this action rhyme. Final translation provided with thanks from Lorraine (Te Rohe) Johnston, Māori Resources Librarian at the University of Otago.

Page 10 China *Little Friends, Hand in Hand*
Kindly recommended and translated by Nora Yao, Director of Confucius Institute, The University of Auckland.

Page 12 Australia *Grandfather*
For Grandad Ken. Kindly donated by Rob Amery, Linguistics, University of Adelaide and Chester Schultz. This is an Aboriginal rhyme in the Kaurna language of the Adelaide Plains. Ngarrindjeri version (Pakanu) by Ruby Hammond & Rob Amery 1990. Kaurna version by Rob Amery, 1995. This song appears on page 15 of Chester Schultz, Nelson Varcoe & Rob Amery eds. (1999) *Kaurna Paltinna* – a Kaurna song book. Published by the editors in Adelaide.

Page 14 Norway *Rain*
With special thanks to Dr. Art Trond Haugen (Subject Librarian, Norwegian and Scandinavian Literature, The National Library, Oslo) for researching and selecting this poem by early modernist poet Sigbjørn Obstfelder. The poem is from a collection called *Poems*, issued in 1893. The English translation is adapted from Paul Selver's version in *A European Anthology* located in *The New Age*, No 1338, Vol XXIV, No 24, Thursday April 17, 1919.

Page 16 Ireland *The Little Donkey*
Kindly received from Máire Ní Chonalláin, Duty Librarian of the National Library of Ireland with special thanks. Thanks also to David Todd and Berni Campbell for their research into copyright.

Page 18 Tonga *Spotty Spider*
Thanks to Wanda Cowley for her translation and permission to use an excerpt from her poem, *The Bargain*, first published in *School Journal* Part 2 Number 3 1983.

Thanks also to Don Long, Ala Toetuu, Selina Tusitala Marsh and Edgar Tu'inukuafe for their help.

Page 20 Jamaica *Tingalay-o!*
Thanks to Julie Sperring for supplying this rhyme and to Xavier Murphy and all at www.jamaicans.com who helped with this version.

Page 22 Japan *Song of Kites*
For Madison Taylor. Thanks to the Japan Information and Culture Center of the Embassy of Japan, in Washington, for supplying this traditional Japanese song (English version abridged).

Page 24 Zimbabwe *Beautiful Bird*
For Archie Walker. Thanks to Winifred Mahowa, Ethnic Advisor, Office of Ethnic Affairs and her mother-in-law Mrs Mavis Kumbula-Mutisi for supplying this traditional nursery rhyme from Zimbabwe in Shona and English translation.

Page 26 Fiji *Tapioca*
Kindly told to me by Ms Seta Monolagi of the Fiji Visitor's Bureau in Auckland. It is an old nursery rhyme taught to her by her mother. Thanks to Sereima Lumelume for the translation.

Page 28 Indonesia *My Village*
Translated by Aida Nofrita from AUT University Certificate in Translation Studies from a famous kindergarten song in Indonesia. Thanks to Ineke Creeze for arranging the translation.

Page 30 Denmark *Snowman Frost*
Kindly sourced by Annette Tjerrild from Aarhus Public Library, Denmark, from a poem by Halfdan Rasmussen with the English translation sourced from a book called *Halfdanes Verse – Sense and Nonsense* by Halfdan Rasmussen. Thanks to Halfdan's daughter Iben Nagel Rasmussen for her assistance and Annette Skovgaard at Copydan for help with clearance.

Page 32 Iran *Let's Play*
Thank you to author Farideh Khalatbaree and Shabaviz Publications in Tehran for supplying this poem (abridged). www.shabaviz.com

Page 34 Germany *Dance, Little One, Dance!*
English translation of this traditional children's song
courtesy of Monique Palomares of
www.mamalise.com/fr

Page 36 Samoa *Savalivali*
Thanks to www.samoaworld.com participants and to
Selina Tusitala Marsh for arranging an edit of the
translation and to Theresa Koroivulaono for her
editing.

Page 38 Switzerland *Joggeli, Can You Ride?*
Thanks to Andrea Gardi and her son Melino for
supplying this traditional rhyme.

Page 40 Russia *Hush You Mice*
All three versions kindly supplied by Genia Gurarie of
Princeton University Alumni with special thanks.

Page 42 Brazil *If This Street Were Mine*
For William. Thanks to Carim Portella for the translation
from Portuguese and for this traditional song from her
homeland.

Page 44 France *What is My Hand Doing?*
A traditional French children's song; thanks to
Lisa Yanucci (www.mamalisa.com) for supplying the
translation. Thanks also to Pat and Paul Wright, and
their neighbour Jean-Louie for help with these rhymes.

Page 46 Holland *Kortjakje is Always Sick*
Thanks to Wilma van den Bosch and Katrien Vander
Straeten for their translations and guidance.

Page 48 Iceland *Bye, Bye, Blacking*
Special thanks to Stefania Anorsdottir, Reference
Librarian at the National and University Library of
Iceland for sourcing this traditional Icelandic lullaby.
Many thanks also to Kirstin and Sigfidur at the Iceland
Music Information Centre for help with credits and
translations and to Ragnheidur Tryggvadottir from the
Icelandic Writers Union for help with copyright
clearance. Thanks also to the Icelandic poet, Hallberg
Hallmundsson, for help with this translation.

Page 50 India *Bathtime*
Translated by Anjana Mani from a traditional rhyme
told to her by her mother Ramila Mani.

We have done everything we
can to track down the original
copyright holders and are reliant
on our translators and editors for
final approval on text translations.
We welcome your input if there are any
discrepancies with text or if you are the
original copyright holder of any of the
rhymes, we would welcome an email to:
flcb@frances-lincoln.com

Thanks to all the people who contributed rhymes not
used in this book.

Finally, thanks to the encouragement of Michelia Ward
(Trade Aid), Carolyne Jurriaans and Joris de Bres (New
Zealand Human Rights Commission), to Julie and
Colleen at Jabberwocky Children's Bookshop, to editor
Penelope Todd, to Caroline Thomson at Arenaworks and
the brilliant Mique Moriuchi for making the words come
to life; and to Michael Rosen for making time in a very
hectic Children's Laureate year to write our introduction.

Thanks also to Julia Marshall (Gecko Press) without
whom this book would not exist.

Thanks mostly though to Gavin and Henry, for
everything else!

Danielle Wright